J

Freschet, Berniece.

Bernard and the Catnip caper

BERNARD
and the
CATNIP CAPER

by
Berniece Freschet

Pictures by Gina Freschet

Charles Scribner's Sons · New York

Text copyright © 1981 Berniece Freschet
Illustrations copyright © 1981 Gina Freschet

Library of Congress Cataloging in Publication Data
Freschet, Berniece.
Bernard and the Catnip caper.
Summary: When the quietest, sleepiest, most timid cat in Boston
is catnapped, a ransom note is sent to Bernard the mouse.
[1. Mice—Fiction. 2. Cats—Fiction. 3. Mystery and detective
stories] I. Freschet, Gina.
II. Title.
PZ7.F88968Bc [E] 81-5322
ISBN 0-684-17157-0 AACR2
1 3 5 7 9 11 13 15 17 19 QD/C 20 18 16 14 12 10 8 6 4 2

Printed in the United States of America

For our brave Sandra

CATNIP IS CATNAPPED

Bernard lived in an old brownstone house at the top of Beacon Hill in Boston, Massachusetts.

He lived there with his father and mother, and his three sisters—Rosie, Cecile, and Poppy—and his two brothers—Ernest and Henry (who were always getting into mischief).

It wasn't as though Bernard had never been outside of Boston. Goodness, no. He had traveled far, and had had many exciting adventures, but for now he was content just to stay at home and relax. The greatest excitement in his life these days was looking after his vegetable garden in the mornings (his squashes were particularly fine) and taking his usual afternoon walk through the Boston Garden.

The rest of the time Bernard spent in his favorite chair in the library of the old house, reading.

It was a good life, calm—quiet—peaceful.

CRASH!

...there was the sound of breaking glass.

Bernard's peaceful quiet was suddenly shattered!

A rock had crashed through the window,
landing right at
his feet.

"I suppose this has something to do with Ernest and Henry,"
Bernard said with a sigh. He smoothed out a piece
of paper tied to the rock and read:

we have
your friend,
CATNIP
put a sack of
CLAMS (shells
removed, please)
IN A plain paper
BAG and put it
under the last seat
OF swanboat #3
in Boston Garden
at nightfall OR
ELSE! you'll never
see your friend again

"Great granddad's whiskers!! Catnip? Catnapped?? Why,
he's the quietest, sleepiest, most timid cat in the world—
you hardly know he's around. A bit dull really.
A nice enough cat, all right—but D-U-L-L.

"Now if it were Tiger II who had been catnapped, I wouldn't worry. He's the exact opposite of Catnip. Those two are as different as night and day, or in this case as different as inside from outside." (Catnip was the inside cat, while Tiger II much preferred being the outside cat.)

"That Tiger II is always on the go, getting into one scrape after another. He leads a very exciting life—at times even dangerous."

Bernard nodded, "Yes, I could see Tiger II getting into trouble, but poor, timid, dull ole Catnip—why, he must be frightened out of his skin."

Bernard frowned and scratched an ear. "This
is a puzzle—yes, a most puzzling puzzle.
Maybe the catnappers have their cats mixed up."

Bernard began to feel the old excitement of an
adventure. He jumped down from his chair.
"Ernest, Henry," called Bernard. "Rosie, Cecile,
Poppy—*come at once.*"

Bernard didn't know it, but his calm—quiet—
peaceful life had just come to an end.

* * *

"Honest, Bernard, we didn't have anything to do with it," Ernest said.

"That's right," agreed Henry. "It wasn't us who threw the rock—we spent the morning helping the girls cook up a new recipe of Welsh Rarebit."

"Having had extensive experience with various kinds of cheeses, we gave them our expert opinion and advice," said Ernest.

Cecile, Rosie, and Poppy nodded in agreement.

"It's absolutely delicious," said Ernest and Henry, licking cheese crumbs from their whiskers.

Bernard tugged on an ear. "We have a very serious matter here. If this isn't a joke, then Catnip is really catnapped."

"Poor Catnip," Rosie sniffed. "He always left me a sip of his morning cream. I hope he isn't hungry."

"He always purred me to sleep whenever I had a bad dream," said Poppy, a tear rolling down her cheek. "I hope he isn't afraid."

"We had such fun when he used to swing us on his tail," Cecile said, blowing her nose. "Being catnapped can't be much fun."

"Sure it is," said Henry. "I bet ole Catnip is having the greatest adventure of his life."

"Well," said Bernard, "let's go see Tiger II. He might know what this is all about. Come along, everyone."

TIGER II

Tiger II read the catnappers' note and began to
chuckle. "What kind of a joke is this? I'll bet
Ernest and Henry had a hand in this. You
guys sure have some imagination," said the big
cat, yowling with laughter.

"It wasn't us," cried Ernest and Henry.

"Ah, come on," said Tiger II. "This can't be for
real—Catnip in a jam?" Tiger II grinned,
showing a chipped tooth. "Now, if it was me
that was catnapped, I could believe it. There's
a few I could name who'd love to get their
paws and claws on me, all right. Not much
chance of that, though," he said, licking a
sharp claw.

Bernard felt a tingle in his tail. Tiger II certainly looked as if he could handle most any situation.

"What about this note?" asked Bernard.

Everyone looked hopefully at Tiger II, since he was the only one with some experience in these matters.

The big cat looked thoughtful. "Well, if this note is on the level, poor ole Catnip could be in a real pickle." Tiger II flicked out a shiny claw. "I'll ask around the waterfront and get back to you at sundown. Meet me at the garden wall." In the blink of a mouse eye, the big cat disappeared as quietly as a shadow.

"All right," said Bernard. "Let's get going. Rosie, Cecile, and Poppy—you go to the fish market and get a sack of clams."
The girls hurried off.

"Ernest, Henry—we'll have to figure out what we'll need to take on this nighttime adventure. Any ideas?"

"How about rope?" suggested Henry.

"We might have to go by water," Ernest said.
"Maybe we should have a raft or boat."

"Good thinking, boys," said Bernard. "You go
and see what you can find."
The two of them raced off.
Bernard paced up and down. "This could be
dangerous. We'd better take weapons to defend
ourselves, just in case. Let's see—ah, I've got
it." In a few minutes he was back in the
library with a package of sewing needles.
"These should do it."

Henry ran into the room carrying a ball of
twine.

"Good work," said Bernard, patting Henry on the back, not recognizing it as the same twine that minutes before had been tied to the bean poles in his vegetable garden.

"Hey, look what I found in the big bathroom," said Ernest, towing a string of bath toys.

"Just the thing," said Bernard. Then he showed them the weapons. "But only to be used if we're attacked," he warned.

The girls came in with the clams.

"The note said that the shells must come off," said Bernard. "While we figure out how to do that, would you girls make some sheaths for the weapons?"

"Sure, Bernard," said the girls. "And let's make a banner to carry into battle."

The next few hours were busy ones.

A ray from the setting sun glinted through the window. Bernard looked up from his work. "It's almost sundown—time to meet Tiger II. I hope he has some news." Everyone hurried outside.

Tiger II was waiting at the garden wall.

"Well?" asked Bernard, "any news?"

"Not a thing," said Tiger II. "I've asked everyone down at the waterfront—but no one has heard a word." He jumped up on the wall and swished his tail back and forth. "This is a real hush-hush caper, or I'd have heard something."

Tiger II looked down at Bernard. "It might be that new gang from the other side of town. They call themselves the Alley Cats and I hear they're a wild bunch."

"Well, the only thing we can do now is to
follow the directions on the note," said
Bernard. "We can't let poor ole Catnip down."
He looked up at Tiger II. "Are you with us?"

"I wouldn't miss it for anything," grinned the
big cat, showing his chipped tooth. "Nothing I
like better than a yowling, howling, good old
free-for-all fight."

Tiger stretched and flexed his muscles. "Are
the girls coming, too?" he asked.

"Of course," said Bernard. "Rosie, Cecile, and Poppy can handle themselves as well or better than any of us—besides, they're very fond of Catnip."

"Well, then," said Tiger II, jumping down, "let's go. And you'd better be ready for a fight. There's not only wild cats out at night, but some pretty tough dogs and rats, too."

A shiver of excitement gripped the younger mice as they all hurried after the big cat.

TO THE RESCUE

The moon came out from behind a cloud.
Black shadows swayed on the garden wall,
showing a little band of determined rescuers
marching down the path. Bernard led—Rosie,
Poppy, and Cecile followed, carrying their
banner. Then came Ernest and Henry, a coil of
twine over their shoulders, and pulling the
string of toy bath floats. Tiger II was last,
carrying the sack of clams.

An hour later Bernard stopped the group in
front of the Swan Boats in Boston Garden.
The night was quiet.
The only sound was the soft swish of water on
the sides of the boats.
The moon shone down on the pond.
High in a tree an owl hooted.
The little group shivered.

"Look at the mooring rope on boat number 3,"
whispered Bernard. "Most of it is under water.
It's a good thing we've got the floats. It's the
only way we can get onto the boat."

They put the floats into the water, and the
mice jumped on—but not Tiger II.
"I'll climb a tree and leap down on the boat
from there," he said.

The floats bobbed silently along in the water.
Softly the little band of rescuers paddled to the
boat. When they came close to the mooring
rope, Ernest and Henry threw the twine up
and over the rope. Everyone climbed up the
twine and ran along the rope to the boat.

The mice dropped down onto the deck.
They huddled together.
"Come on," whispered Bernard.
Slowly, they tiptoed forward.
Suddenly, out of the blackness,
a shadow leaped down at them.
They crouched, their weapons drawn.

It was only Tiger II jumping from the limb.
"You gave us quite a start," whispered Bernard.
"Sorry," said the big cat, "but there was no way
  to warn you."

Tiger II put the sack of clams under the last
seat of the Swan Boat.
Everyone hid. They watched—and waited.

Nearby a board creaked. There was a muffled
sound of someone moving close. A shadowy
paw reached out of the darkness and picked
up the sack of clams.

Bernard jumped out. "Stop where you are."
The others followed, their weapons raised.

"WAIT—it's me—*Catnip!*"

"CATNIP?" Everyone talked at once—"Where did you come from?"—"Did you escape?"— "Where are the catnappers?"

"Hold on," said Bernard. "Let's find out what's going on here. Catnip, you look awful. Are you all right? We've been very worried about you."

Catnip's fur was rumpled and dirty. He looked as if he hadn't slept in days. "I'm all right," said Catnip. "I'm just a bit worn out, and very hungry—have you got the clams?" He reached into the sack and took a big bite of one.

"How did you know there were clams
in that sack?" asked Bernard.
Catnip looked sheepish. "Well—"
But before he could finish—

Dark figures came out of the shadows, facing
the little group.

"Wh—who are yo—you?" stuttered Bernard.

"We're the Alley Cats," said the biggest,
meanest-looking cat that the mice had ever
seen in all their lives.

"And this is our territory. You'd better have a good reason for being on our turf." The leader jumped in front of Tiger II. "And just who are you?" he hissed.

"Tiger II," hissed back Tiger.

The leader snarled, "Hey, gang—look who we've got here—the famous Tiger II. We've heard of you all right." The gang of cats circled around Tiger. "Yeah, we've heard you're pretty tough. Okay, gang, let's see just how tough this cat is."

With every eye on Tiger II, Bernard decided that now was the time to make his move. "CHARGE!" he shouted, and he lead the mouse band into battle.

They fought bravely. The mouse girls were
quick, and expert…
…the boys were daring—sometimes a bit too
daring.

Bernard seemed to be everywhere at once,
parrying, and thrusting, and shouting words of
encouragement.

Even Catnip joined in.
It was Catnip who saw Henry fall overboard
into the water. Without thinking, he jumped in,
picked up Henry, and put him on the duck.

Tiger II was in the middle of the brawl—with
batting paws—and slashing claws—
But the band of rescuers was greatly
outnumbered, and it looked like a losing battle.

Suddenly, from the tree limbs above—
screeching bodies leaped down onto the boat.

"It's my friends from the waterfront!" shouted
Tiger II.

The air became filled with the sound of
spitting, growling, hissing, yowling cats. It was
what Tiger II called a good old free-for-all fight.
Soon the Alley Cats were scrambling off
the boat in every direction.

After much hearty back-slapping and joyous congratulations on their victory, Tiger II and the mouse family took Catnip home.

When they were safe inside the old brownstone house, and Catnip was fed and washed, everyone clamored to hear his story.

"This whole thing was all my fault," said Catnip. "I wrote the note and then hid out in the boat."

"But why?" asked Bernard. "Why did you pretend to be catnapped?"

"Because I was bored with my life," said
Catnip. "Everyone here has had some
adventure in his life, but nothing
has ever happened to me."
Everyone looked surprised.

"And do you know why my life was so
boring?" asked Catnip. "Because I was
afraid—afraid to leave the house. One day I
just got sick and tired of being dull, boring,
scared ole Catnip—so I thought up this
catnapping thing, only it got a bit out of hand.
I'm sorry."
Catnip looked very sorry indeed.

"Well, it proved one thing," said Tiger II,
looking a bit uncomfortable at being inside the
house. "You're not the coward you
thought—you did rescue Henry."

"And it did make us appreciate all the nice
things you do for us," said Rosie, Cecile, and
Poppy.

"And it sure was a terrific adventure," said
Ernest and Henry.

"Well, I've learned my lesson," said Catnip,
licking a sore paw. "I've had enough
adventure. Those Alley Cats are a mean bunch.
I never want to leave the house again—
no matter how dull and boring I become."

"I've learned something myself tonight," said
Bernard. "A little adventure is good—it
sharpens one's wits." He picked up his book
and settled back into his chair.
"But most important—it makes us realize how nice
a little peace and quiet can be."